Library of Congress Cataloging in Publication Data:
Cosgrove, Stephen. Chatterbox. (A Whimsie storybook) SUMMARY: Switch Witch causes Bluebell to become so talkative that no one wants to be around her.   1. Children's stories, American.
[1. Listening—Fiction.   2. Witches—Fiction]   I. Reasoner, Charles, ill.   II. Title.
III. Series: Cosgrove, Stephen. Whimsie storybook.   PZ7.C8187Ch   1985   [E]
85-42714   ISBN: 0-394-87456-0

Manufactured in Belgium
1 2 3 4 5 6 7 8 9 0

The Whimsies™ STORYBOOKS

Chatterbox

by Stephen Cosgrove

illustrated by Charles Reasoner

Random House New York

Have you ever lost a kite on a windy day and sadly watched it fly away? If you could follow that kite high above the clouds and sail beyond your fondest wish, you would find the Land of Whim.

In this land of soft breezes lived furry little creatures called Whimsies. The Whimsies had cute button noses and bright, shiny eyes, and were covered from head to foot with fur as soft as dandelion down.

As the Whimsies went about their village doing their dail chores, occasionally they would stop to chat with one ar other.

They would listen attentively to what the other had t say and then bustle on their way. For the Whimsies wer the best and most polite listeners in all the Land of Whim

One little Whimsie was named Bluebell, and like all the others, she loved to listen to everything around her. It was her job to walk through Forever Forest and collect branches of fragrant juniper and pine for firewood. Along the way Bluebell would stop and listen to the birds singing their songs.

Bluebell would listen to the chattering squirrels who lived in the woods. The squirrels were the biggest gossips any-where in this magical land, but Bluebell liked to listen to all that they had to say and then go quietly on her way.

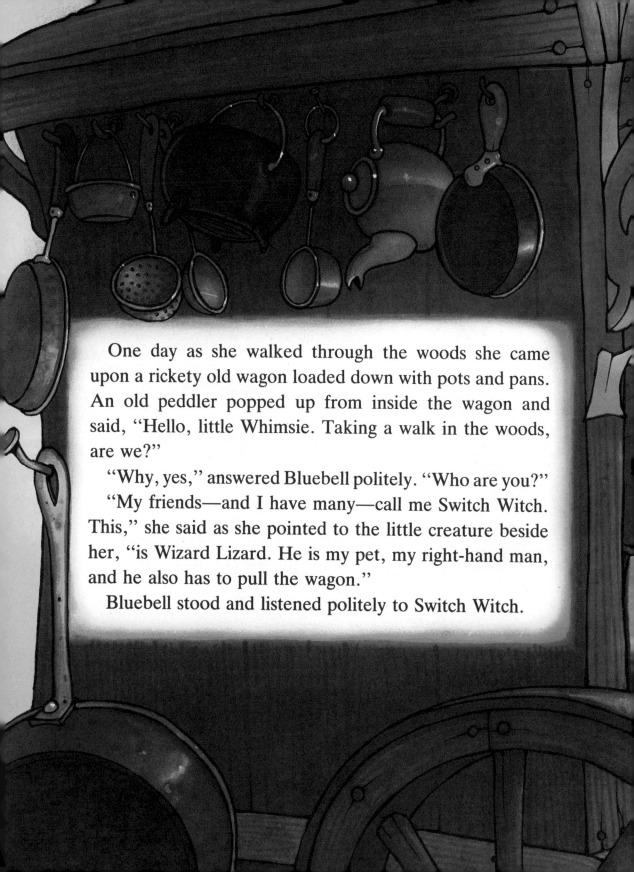

One day as she walked through the woods she came upon a rickety old wagon loaded down with pots and pans. An old peddler popped up from inside the wagon and said, "Hello, little Whimsie. Taking a walk in the woods, are we?"

"Why, yes," answered Bluebell politely. "Who are you?"

"My friends—and I have many—call me Switch Witch. This," she said as she pointed to the little creature beside her, "is Wizard Lizard. He is my pet, my right-hand man, and he also has to pull the wagon."

Bluebell stood and listened politely to Switch Witch.

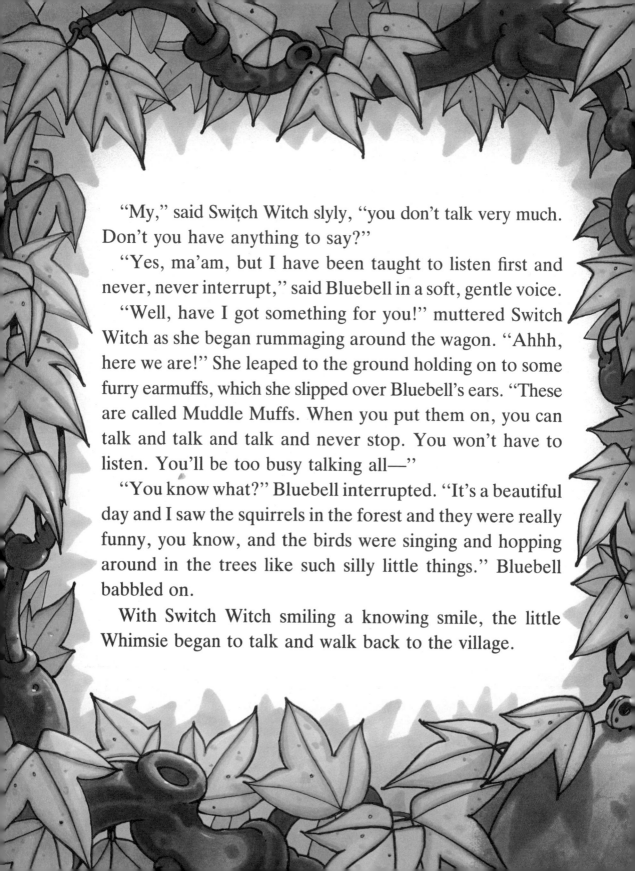

"My," said Switch Witch slyly, "you don't talk very much. Don't you have anything to say?"

"Yes, ma'am, but I have been taught to listen first and never, never interrupt," said Bluebell in a soft, gentle voice.

"Well, have I got something for you!" muttered Switch Witch as she began rummaging around the wagon. "Ahhh, here we are!" She leaped to the ground holding on to some furry earmuffs, which she slipped over Bluebell's ears. "These are called Muddle Muffs. When you put them on, you can talk and talk and talk and never stop. You won't have to listen. You'll be too busy talking all—"

"You know what?" Bluebell interrupted. "It's a beautiful day and I saw the squirrels in the forest and they were really funny, you know, and the birds were singing and hopping around in the trees like such silly little things." Bluebell babbled on.

With Switch Witch smiling a knowing smile, the little Whimsie began to talk and walk back to the village.

On the way down the path Bluebell chattered on and on. She talked the pollen off the flowers and the leaves right off the trees. The squirrels, though they tried and tried, couldn't get a word in edgewise. Bluebell didn't care, for she loved the sound of her own voice. What a chatterbox she had become!

Bluebell raced into the village talking a mile a minute. She interrupted a group of Whimsies who were discussing the weather to tell them what had happened in school nearly a week ago.

And she interrupted some Whimsie children who were playing to tell them what she had seen in Forever Forest.

"You know what I just saw?" she chattered. "The flowers danced in the wind and the air smelled beautiful and the sky was so cloudy and the path was windy in Forever Forest . . . ."

The Whimsie children all put their hands over their ears and said, "What a chatterbox you are, Bluebell."

After Bluebell had nearly talked the ears off all the Whimsies in the street, she rushed home to eat her lunch.

Without so much as an "Excuse me!" or a "By your leave," she interrupted her parents, who were sitting at the table having a pleasant chat.

"You know what?" said Bluebell. "I'm so hungry I could eat a whale. No, I wouldn't eat a whale, 'cause whales are

so kind, but I'm so hungry I could eat a zillion bowls of dandelion soup. Boy, that must make me the hungriest Whimsie in the whole world . . . ."

Her father tried to ask her to be quiet. Her mother tried to find out why she was wearing those strange earmuffs on such a warm day. But they couldn't slip a single word in when Bluebell was talking.

"Why has Bluebell become such an unbearable chatter-box?" her mother wondered. And she decided to go see Grandma Whimsie, one of the oldest and wisest Whimsies. Perhaps she could be of help.

Bluebell's mother found Grandma at the dock.

"I can't stand it. Bluebell babbles on and on!" she told Grandma Whimsie.

Grandma Whimsie knew what the problem was right away. "Switch Witch has given her the Muddle Muffs!" she said. "The only way to remove the spell is for Bluebell to listen to her own heart. From now on, no matter what she has to say, no Whimsie is to listen and instead must walk away."

Bluebell's mother told everyone in the village what Grandma Whimsie said. From that moment on, whenever Bluebell the chatterbox appeared, the other Whimsies would stop talking and quietly walk away. At first she didn't even notice as she babbled on, talking only to herself. But as the day wore on she began to feel lonelier and lonelier.

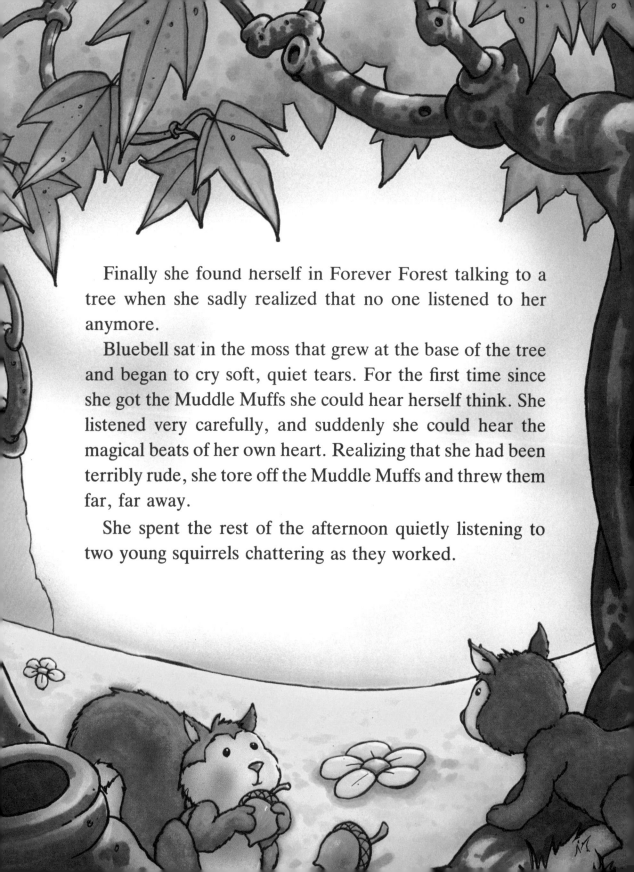

Finally she found herself in Forever Forest talking to a tree when she sadly realized that no one listened to her anymore.

Bluebell sat in the moss that grew at the base of the tree and began to cry soft, quiet tears. For the first time since she got the Muddle Muffs she could hear herself think. She listened very carefully, and suddenly she could hear the magical beats of her own heart. Realizing that she had been terribly rude, she tore off the Muddle Muffs and threw them far, far away.

She spent the rest of the afternoon quietly listening to two young squirrels chattering as they worked.

The Muddle Muffs lay quietly in the moss and would have been there to this very day had it not been for Switch Witch and Wizard Lizard, who were out searching for toadstools. Curiously the little lizard picked up the earmuffs, and before the old witch could stop him, he popped them on his head.

Just like that, Wizard Lizard began to babble on and on about how mean Switch Witch was. Switch Witch was trapped by his words and had to listen to his endless chatter as he pulled the old wagon back to the Land of Frippery.

From that day forward Bluebell listened when others spoke and only spoke when she had something to say.

You can talk all you want,
But you should listen, too!
Just remember the lesson
Bluebell taught to you.